DISCOVER
DESIERTO

Spanish Edition

x*ist Publishing

Planta de Agave

Planta de Aloe

Águila Calva

Bellos Cactus

Cactus en Flor

Gato Montés

Cactus

Fruto de Cactus

Camello

Coyote

Casa del Desierto

Tortuga del Desierto

Águila Real

Serpiente de Gopher

Liebre

Lagartija

Cardo de Leche

Serpiente de Cascabel de Mojave

Codorniz

Serpiente de Cascabel

Correcaminos

Esfinge

Rodadora

Published in the United States by Xist Publishing
www.xistpublishing.com
PO Box 61593 Irvine, CA 92602
© 2017 Spanish Edition by Xist Publishing
All rights reserved
This has been translated by Victor Santana.
No portion of this book may be reproduced without express permission of the publisher
All images licensed from Fotolia
© 2012 by Xist Publishing First Edition

ISBN-13: 9781532403934 • eISBN: 9781532403941

xist Publishing

Made in United States
Orlando, FL
07 July 2024